Lizzie Mcknight

Illustrations By:

Candyce Marsh John

S0-BDO-299

To my Ladybug

Love is more than a word....Love is an action.
....Children should be able to see, hear, and
feel it in every way, everyday.

Mama, do you love me?

Of course, my love.

How do I know you love me?

Mama takes a moment, points to the sky and asks....

What color is the sky?

Blue and white!

Well, how do you know?....

....Because I can see it!

....That's right, Wonderful!

Mama, do you love me?

Of course I do, my love.

How do I know?

YeeEEEeeess, I shiver, as mama buttons up my warm coat.

Is it chilly today?

Yes! I nod.

Well, how do you know?

Because I can feel it! The cool air on my face, and the goosebumps on my arms!.... Thank goodness you brought my coat!

That's right! Mama replies.

Mama, do you love me?

Of course my love.

How do I know?

Mama scoops me up in her arms and squeezes tight.

What am I doing?

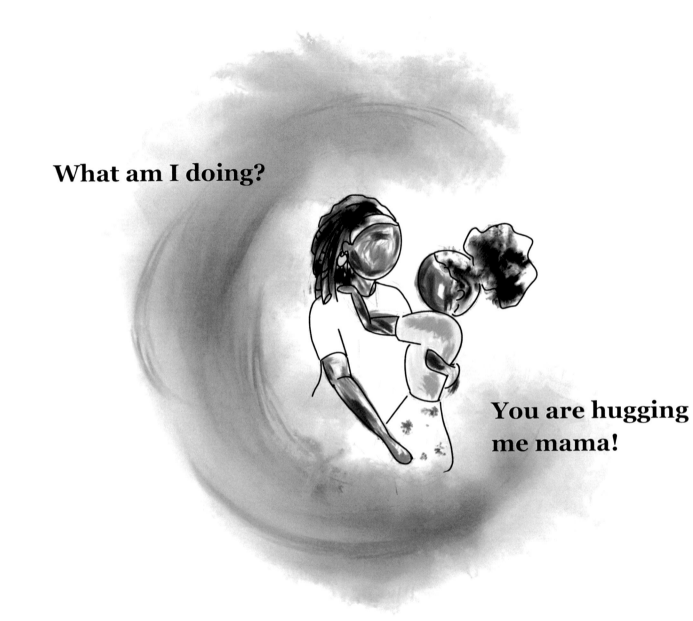

You are hugging me mama!

How do you
know?

Because I can feel your
arms around me.

Daddy walks in from work and I run into his arms!

He scoops me up and asks me why I am so excited.

Because Daddy, I know that you love me!

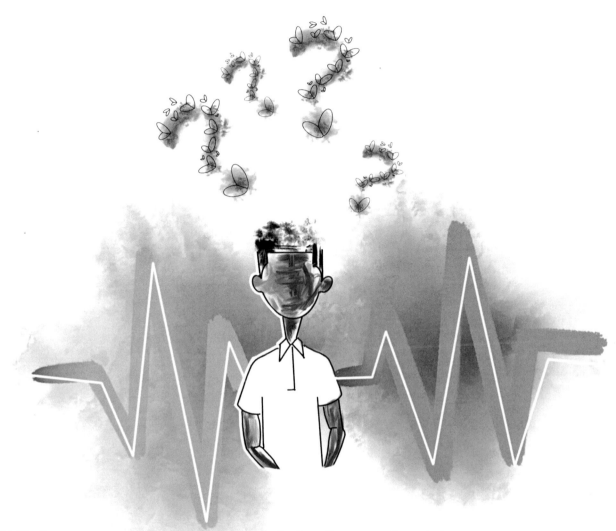

With a puzzled look on his face, daddy asks....How do you Know?

I see it when you kiss my boo boos...
and make them feel better.

And make my favorite lunch...

I hear it when we sing together....

And during our prayers at night.... When we thank God for all of our blessings.

Most of all, I feel it right here.

Mama and Daddy asks, "Where's that?

My Heart! I feel all of your love in my heart!

That is how I know
you love me....and I
love you too!

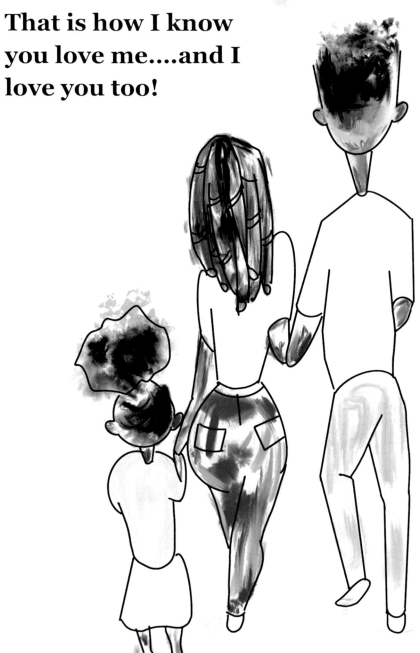

Draw a self portrait!

Draw your family!

Made in United States
North Haven, CT
28 December 2021

13808958R00018